Books sho...
above. Re
www.kent.

_____

____

L

Old Mother Hubbard

Retold by Russell Punter

Illustrated by Fred Blunt

Reading consultant: Alison Kelly
Roehampton University

Old Mother Hubbard
went to the cupboard,

to fetch her poor doggie
a bone.

But when she got there,
the cupboard was bare.

And so the poor doggie
had none.

Old Mother Hubbard
shut up the cupboard

and put on her warm
winter clothes.

"We'll have to go out," she said with a shout,

"before all the butchers
are closed."

So off down the lane,
through wind and
through rain,

went Old Mother
Hubbard and Spot.

'Til they came to a stop,
at Bob's Butcher's Shop.

And they went in to see what was what.

Bob the Butcher

There was plenty of
meat, for a doggie-sized
treat,

but the old lady picked
out a bone.

Then came the snag,
when she looked in
her bag –

she had left all her
money at home.

The pair stepped outside.
"Stop thief!" came
Bob's cry.

Bob the Butche

And a man hurried by
in a flash.

He ran with such
speed, he tripped on
Spot's lead.

And went flying, along
with the cash.

Bob the Butcher

"Your dog stopped that thief," said Bob with relief.

Bob the Butche

"So I must reward you, my dear."

Now Old Mother
Hubbard has a very
full cupboard.

And her doggie has
best steak all year.

Puzzles

Puzzle 1

Can you spot the differences
between these two pictures?
There are six to find.

27

Puzzle 2
Find these things in
the picture:

dog   clock   cupboard

window   cup   kettle

Puzzle 3
Choose the best sentence
for each picture.

29

Answers to puzzles

Puzzle 1

Puzzle 2

clock   cupboard   window

kettle   cup   dog

Puzzle 3

I'm wet.

Stop thief!

Series editor: Lesley Sims

SPOT

First published in 2010 by Usborne Publishing Ltd., Usborne House,
83-85 Saffron Hill, London EC1N 8RT, England. www.usborne.com
Copyright © 2010 Usborne Publishing Ltd.

32